D1110075

A Note to Parents and Caregivers:

Read-it! Readers are for children who are just starting on the amazing road to reading. These beautiful books support both the acquisition of reading skills and the love of books.

 The PURPLE LEVEL presents basic topics and objects using high frequency words and simple language patterns.

 The RED LEVEL presents familiar topics using common words and repeating sentence patterns.

 The BLUE LEVEL presents new ideas using a larger vocabulary and varied sentence structure.

 The YELLOW LEVEL presents more challenging ideas, a broad vocabulary, and wide variety in sentence structure.

 The GREEN LEVEL presents more complex ideas, an extended vocabulary range, and expanded language structures.

 The ORANGE LEVEL presents a wide range of ideas and concepts using challenging vocabulary and complex language structures.

When sharing a book with your child, read in short stretches, pausing often to talk about the pictures. Have your child turn the pages and point to the pictures and familiar words. And be sure to reread favorite stories or parts of stories.

There is no right or wrong way to share books with children. Find time to read with your child, and pass on the legacy of literacy.

Adria F. Klein, Ph.D.
Professor Emeritus
California State University
San Bernardino, California

Editor: Patricia Stockland
Page Production: Melissa Kes/JoAnne Nelson/Tracy Davies
Art Director: Keith Griffin
Managing Editor: Catherine Neitge
The illustrations in this book were rendered digitally.

Picture Window Books
5115 Excelsior Boulevard
Suite 232
Minneapolis, MN 55416
877-845-8392
www.picturewindowbooks.com

Printed in the United States of America.

Library of Congress Cataloging-in-Publication Data
Blair, Eric.
The gingerbread man / by Eric Blair ; illustrated by Ben Peterson.
p. cm. — (Read-it! readers folk tales)
Summary: A freshly baked gingerbread man escapes when he is taken out of the oven
and eludes a number of pursuers until he meets a clever fox.
ISBN 1-4048-0969-4 (hardcover) (reinforced library binding: alk. paper)
[1. Fairy tales. 2. Folklore.] I. Peterson, Ben, ill. II. Title. III. Series: Read-it! readers
folk tales.
PZ8.B5688Gi 2004
398.21—dc22   2004018434

The Gingerbread Man

By Eric Blair

Illustrated by Ben Peterson

Special thanks to our advisers for their expertise:

Adria F. Klein, Ph.D.
Professor Emeritus, California State University
San Bernardino, California

Susan Kesselring, M.A.
Literacy Educator
Rosemount-Apple Valley-Eagan (Minnesota) School District

PICTURE WINDOW BOOKS
Minneapolis, Minnesota

A little old woman and a little old man lived together in a little old house. They had no children, but they wanted one.

One day, the little old woman made a gingerbread boy. "Now I shall have a boy of my own," she thought.

When the gingerbread boy was done baking, he jumped off the pan and ran out the door. The little old woman and the little old man ran after him.

The gingerbread boy laughed and shouted, "Run, run, as fast as you can. You can't catch me. I'm the gingerbread man!" And they couldn't catch him.

The gingerbread boy ran until he came to a cow by the road. "Wait, gingerbread boy!" said the cow. "I want to eat you."

8

As the cow chased him, the gingerbread boy called, "Run, run, as fast as you can. You can't catch me. I'm the gingerbread man!" And the cow couldn't catch him.

The gingerbread boy ran until he came to a horse in a pasture. "Stop!" the horse cried. "I want to eat you!" The gingerbread boy only laughed.

As the horse chased him, the gingerbread boy called, "Run, run, as fast as you can. You can't catch me. I'm the gingerbread man!" And the horse couldn't catch him.

The gingerbread boy ran until he came to some farmers in a barn. When the farmers smelled him, they cried, "Don't run away, gingerbread boy. We'd like to eat you."

As the farmers chased him, the gingerbread boy called, "Run, run, as fast as you can. You can't catch me. I'm the gingerbread man!" And they couldn't catch him.

The gingerbread boy ran until he came to a group of cowboys. The cowboys shouted, "Slow down! We want to eat you."

When the gingerbread boy was ahead of the cowboys, he called, "Run, run, as fast as you can. You can't catch me. I'm the gingerbread man!" And they couldn't catch him.

15

By then, the gingerbread boy thought no one would ever catch him.

Soon, the gingerbread boy saw a fox coming across a field.

The fox began to run after him. The gingerbread boy ran faster.

The gingerbread boy cried, "You can't catch me!" And he ran away.

The gingerbread boy shouted, "I have run away from a little old woman, a little old man, a cow, a horse, a barn full of farmers, and a group of cowboys. And I can run away from you, too."

The fox said, "I would not catch you if I could. I wouldn't dream of hurting you."

21

Just then, the gingerbread boy came to a river. He could not swim, but he wanted to keep running away from the cow, the horse, and the people.

"Jump onto my tail, and I will take you across," said the fox.

The gingerbread boy jumped onto the fox's tail, and the fox swam into the river.

The fox said, "Gingerbread boy, I think you'd better get onto my back, or you might fall off."

The gingerbread boy climbed onto the fox's back.

After swimming a little farther, the fox said, "Gingerbread boy, I am afraid you will get wet. You'd better get onto my shoulder."

The gingerbread boy stepped onto the
fox's shoulder. A little while later, the fox
said, "Gingerbread boy, my shoulder
is sinking. Will you please jump onto
my nose?"

29

The gingerbread boy jumped onto the fox's nose. When they reached the shore, the fox threw back his head and gobbled up the gingerbread boy.

And that was the end of the
gingerbread boy.

More *Read-it!* Readers

Bright pictures and fun stories help you practice your reading skills. Look for more books at your level.

FOLK TALES

Chicken Little by Christianne C. Jones

The Gingerbread Man by Eric Blair

How Many Spots Does a Leopard Have?
    by Christianne C. Jones

The Little Red Hen by Christianne C. Jones

How the Camel Got Its Hump by Christianne C. Jones

The Pied Piper by Eric Blair

Stone Soup by Christianne C. Jones

Looking for a specific title or level? A complete list of *Read-it!* Readers is available on our Web site: *www.picturewindowbooks.com*